The
Vesuvius Club
Graphic Edition

For MARCUS, GUY and G. I. M.

The Vesuvius Club
Graphic Edition

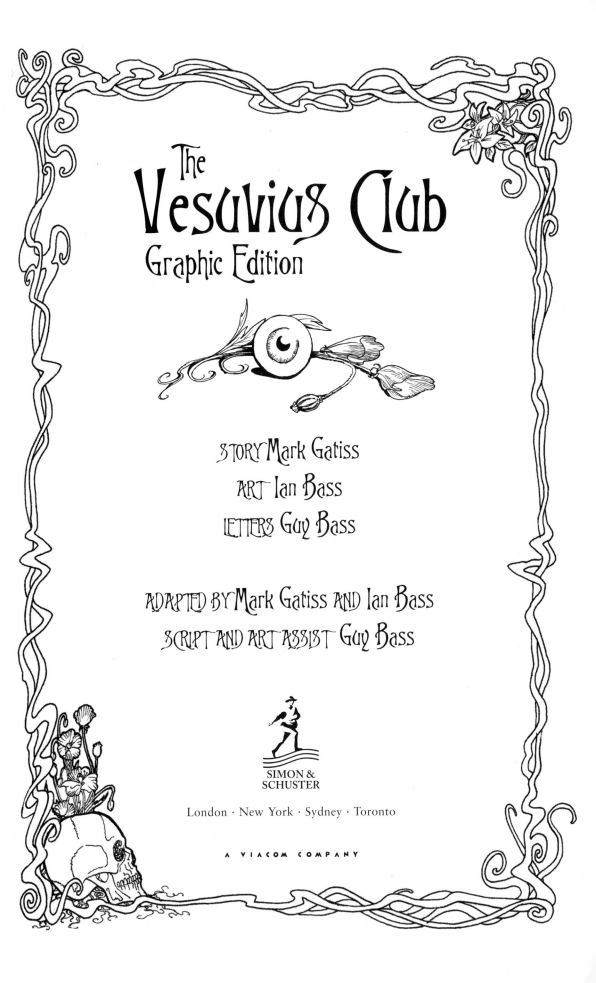

STORY Mark Gatiss

ART Ian Bass

LETTERS Guy Bass

ADAPTED BY Mark Gatiss AND Ian Bass

SCRIPT AND ART ASSIST Guy Bass

SIMON & SCHUSTER

London · New York · Sydney · Toronto

A VIACOM COMPANY

First published in Great Britain by Simon & Schuster UK Ltd, 2005
A Viacom Company

1 3 5 7 9 10 8 6 4 2

Simon & Schuster UK Ltd
Africa House
64-78 Kingsway
London WC2B 6AH

www.simonsays.co.uk

Simon & Schuster Australia
Sydney

A CIP catalogue record for this book
is available from the British Library

ISBN 0-7432-7600-0
EAN 9780743276009

Printed and bound in Great Britain by Scotprint

PART ONE

Mr. Lucifer Box Entertains

London in the summertime.

Hellish. As any resident will tell you.

It smells of roasting excrement.

I know, ostentatious isnt it?

But somebody has to live there!

WHAT A HAPPY ACCIDENT.

JUST THE SHADE OF GREEN I HAD IN MIND FOR A NEW TIE.

GOOD EVENING, DELILAH.

HEVENING, SIR.

HEVERYTHING IN HORDER?

HMMM? OH YES. THE BURGUNDY WAS DREADFUL AND THE PARTRIDGE A TRIFLE HIGH. OTHER THAT THAT A MOST SATISFACTORY EVENING.

AND THE HOTHER GENNLEMAN, SIR?

WILL BE LEAVING US NOW, THANK YOU.

Thus, I assumed the disguise of a dour faced obit writer (false moustache a prerequisite)...

... and went to visit the widow Verdigris at her Holland Park home.

THE PALL MALL GAZETTE OFFERS ITS *SINCEREST* CONDOLENCES.

OH YES, IT WAS SO *UNEXPECTED.* ELI HAS NEVER HAD A DAY'S ILLNESS IN HIS LIFE.

EVEN THE DOCTORS WERE AT SOMETHING OF A *LOSS.*

A *SEIZURE* OF SOME KIND FOLLOWED BY COMA AND... WELL... *DEATH.*

COULD YOU GIVE ME SOME IDEA AS TO THE *NATURE* OF YOUR HUSBAND'S WORK?

OH YES, HERE.

ELI'S *MAGNUM OPUS*.

MAGNETIC VISCOSITY ~ IN ON VOLCANOES ~

YOUR HUSBAND WAS ACQUAINTED WITH THE LATE PROFESSOR *SASH?*

OH YES, FROM THEIR CAMBRIDGE DAYS.

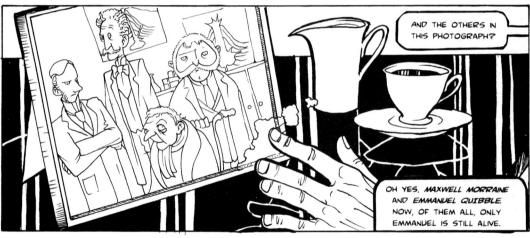

AND THE OTHERS IN THIS PHOTOGRAPH?

OH YES, *MAXWELL MORRAINE* AND *EMMANUEL QUIBBLE*. NOW, OF THEM ALL, ONLY EMMANUEL IS STILL ALIVE.

OF COURSE THERE WAS NO ILL FEELING BETWEEN—

OH *NO.*

SOME PROFESSIONAL RIVALRY, *NATURALLY,* WITH THEM WORKING IN THE SAME FIELD, BUT NOTHING MORE.

THEY HAD SEEN VERY LITTLE OF ONE ANOTHER SINCE THEY ALL WORKED TOGETHER IN EUROPE.

ONE FINAL THING, MRS VERDIGRIS. HAVE I MISSED THE *FUNERAL?*

OH YES. JUST YESTERDAY. THERE AGAIN I WAS *VEXED.*

THE *UNDERTAKING* FIRM THAT MY HUSBAND'S FAMILY HAD ALWAYS RELIED UPON, *RETIRED* WITHOUT SO MUCH AS A NOTE!

THERE WAS SOMETHING A LITTLE *QUEER* ABOUT THEIR REPLACEMENTS. IT WAS A MOST *AMATEURISH* DISPLAY.

AND THE *NAME* OF THIS CURIOUS FIRM?

TOM BOWLER SUPERIOR FUNERALS.

I FOUND THEIR ATTITUDE TO BE MOST *PECULIAR.*

IT WOULD EASE MY MIND IF SOMEONE WERE TO DO A LITTLE...

"DIGGING?"

I returned to Downing Street wondering how to infiltrate an undertakers...

...without a cadaver to present.

16

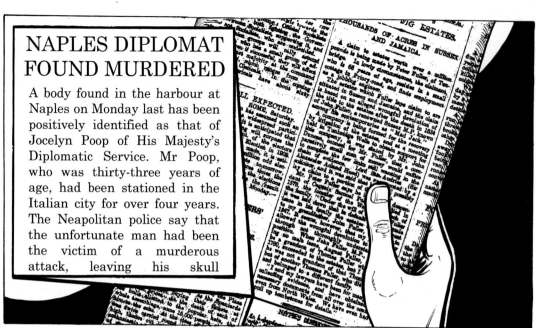

NAPLES DIPLOMAT FOUND MURDERED

A body found in the harbour at Naples on Monday last has been positively identified as that of Jocelyn Poop of His Majesty's Diplomatic Service. Mr Poop, who was thirty-three years of age, had been stationed in the Italian city for over four years. The Neapolitan police say that the unfortunate man had been the victim of a murderous attack, leaving his skull

'AT'S THE ONE YER ARFTER.

With *Verdigris* missing, I took the liberty of having Professor Sash *exhumed*. Once again, I found a *dummy* in place of a body. I was certain of *Tom Bowler's* involvement, but had more pressing matters with which to contend.

Verdigris and Sash... Of the *Cambridge Four*, only Professor *Quibble* remained. It was clear that *Naples* beckoned.

All the nice girls love a *sailor*. That they also like secret servicemen is fortunate as yours truly is no *Jack tar*. Sea voyages have never been my *forte*, but whichever way one looked at it, I was long overdue that European excursion.

Poop, the poor sap... *3 to VC*, Sash, Verdigris... could there be a connection?

Naples...

All roads lead to Naples.

THE HOTEL SANTA LUCIA.

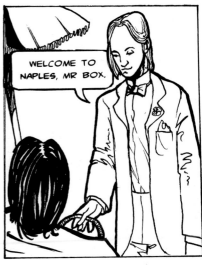

WELCOME TO NAPLES, MR BOX.

Temptation, in this line of work, is *everywhere*. But *time*, dear reader, was of the essence, and pursuits of an *artistic* kind would simply have to wait.

I promised Bella a rendezvous at a more opportune moment...

...and set my mind to *business*.

PROFESSOR *QUIBBLE?*

PROFESSOR... QUIBBLE...

LUCIFER BOX. I HAVE AN APPOINTMENT...

COME...

A TRIFLE *WARM* ISN'T IT?

YES... THE PROFESSOR FEELS THE *COLD* *MOST* TERRIBLY, SIR...

COME... COME....

AND RATHER—

DARK... HIS LORDSHIP DOES NOT CARE FOR THE *LIGHT*.

NO *LAMPS*, NO LAMPS. THAT WILL BE THE DAY... THAT WILL BE THE DAY, AS THEY SAY.

COME...

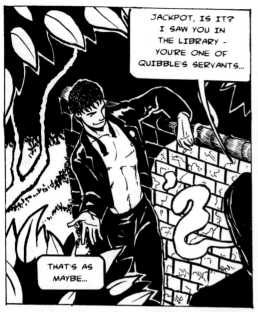

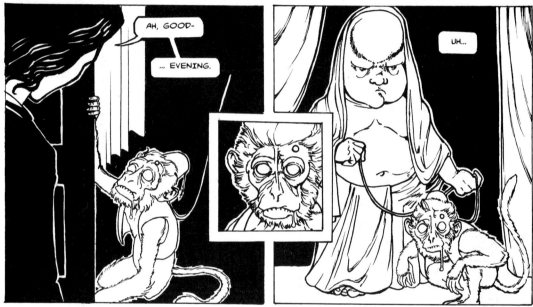

Well of *course* I had noticed... *VC!*
3 to VC. And now here I was.

PART TWO

The Engines of Vulcan

AND THAT'S
THAT.

W-W-WAIT! *WAIT!*
A-*HEH* WHAT ABOUT
ME? I CAN TELL YOU
WHERE YOUR LITTLE
FRIEND IS! YES! *YES!*
HELP ME *HELP* YOU!
A-HEE!

CHARLIE...

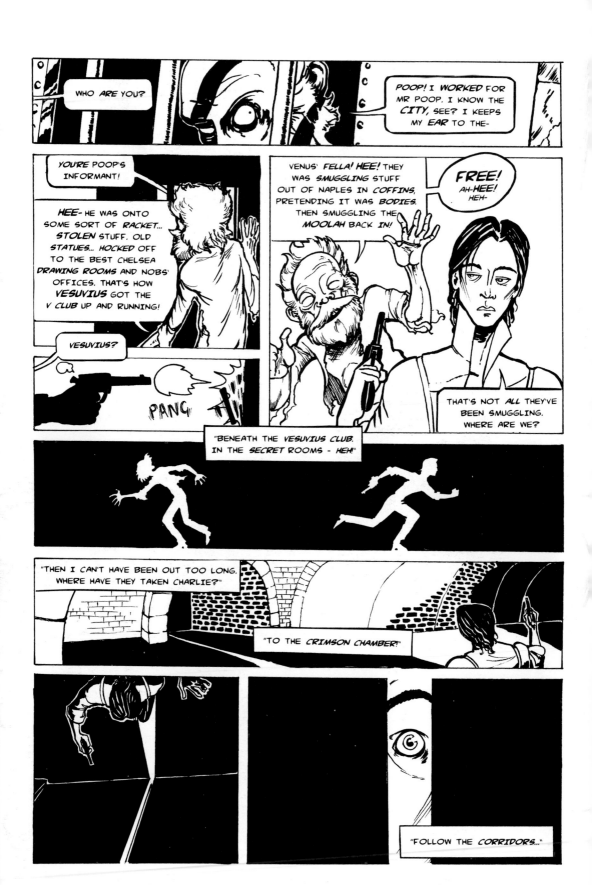

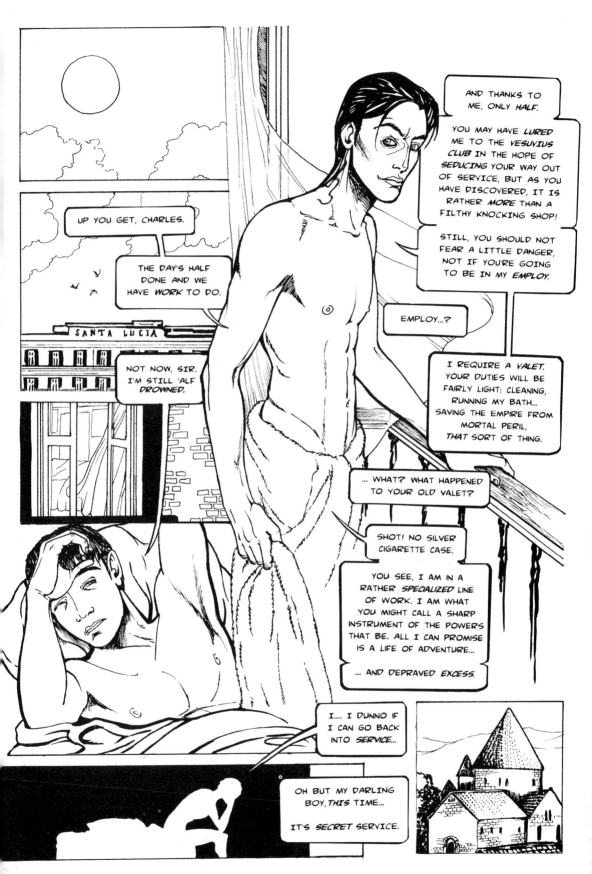

BACK AT THE HOUSE OF PROFESSOR QUIBBLE...

WHAT HAPPENED?

HE'S GONE, SIR... *VANISHED!*

WE WERE RIGHT TO RETURN, CHARLIE. I *TOLD* HIM, BUT HE WOULDN'T LISTEN...

MR *STINT*, ANYTHING UNUSUAL IN HIS BEHAVIOUR?

NO... AS USUAL, AT A QUARTER TO NINE...

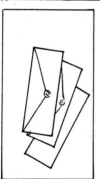

... I BROUGHT HIM HIS *POST.* I RETURNED AT TEN TO BRING HIS *COFFEE...*

... BUT FOUND THE LIBRARY *LOCKED!* WHEN I BROKE DOWN THE DOOR... THE LIBRARY WAS *EMPTY!*

AND HOW DOES A CRIPPLED MAN ESCAPE VIA THE FRENCH WIN—

HELLO, WHAT'S THIS? ONLY THIS *PURPLE* ENVELOPE HAS BEEN OPENED.

YET THERE IS NO *ENCLOSURE.*

THE *FIRE* WAS BURNING?

YES...

SNIF

D'YOU SMELL THAT, CHARLIE?

WHAT'S IT ALL MEAN, MR BOX?

HERE'S WHAT HAPPENED TO PROFESSOR SIR EMMANUEL *QUIBBLE...*

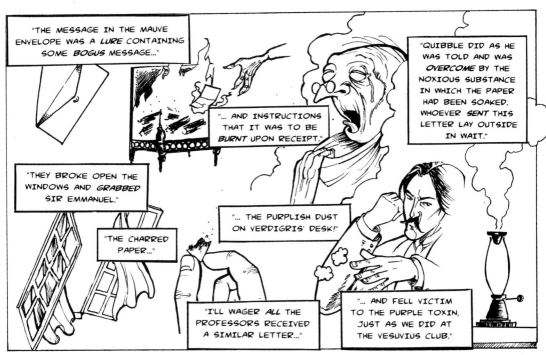

"THE MESSAGE IN THE MAUVE ENVELOPE WAS A *LURE* CONTAINING SOME *BOGUS* MESSAGE..."

"... AND INSTRUCTIONS THAT IT WAS TO BE *BURNT* UPON RECEIPT."

"QUIBBLE DID AS HE WAS TOLD AND WAS *OVERCOME* BY THE NOXIOUS SUBSTANCE IN WHICH THE PAPER HAD BEEN SOAKED. WHOEVER *SENT* THIS LETTER LAY OUTSIDE IN WAIT."

"THEY BROKE OPEN THE WINDOWS AND *GRABBED* SIR EMMANUEL."

"THE CHARRED PAPER..."

"... THE PURPLISH DUST ON VERDIGRIS' DESK!"

"I'LL WAGER *ALL* THE PROFESSORS RECEIVED A SIMILAR LETTER..."

"... AND FELL VICTIM TO THE PURPLE TOXIN, JUST AS WE DID AT THE VESUVIUS *CLUB*."

STINT, WHY DID QUIBBLE BECOME *ENRAGED* AT THE MENTION OF *MAXWELL MORRAINE?*

"MORRAINE... A *TERRIBLE* TRAGEDY, SIR. MORRAINE WENT QUITE... *FUNNY.*"

"THEY SAY IT WAS ON ACCOUNT OF HIS *WIFE* BURNING IN THE *FIRE*..."

HE HAD THEORIES ABOUT HARNESSING THE POWER OF *VOLCANOES*...

VOLCANOES... NO, WE'LL START WITH THIS *PURPLE* CONCOCTION. THIS...

CHARLIE, WHERE WOULD YOU GO FOR THE BEST NARCOTICS IN NAPLES?

KNEW I'D COME IN USEFUL...

THERE'S AN *OPIUM* DEN, THE LARGEST IN THE CITY...

... THAT ZOMBIE IS PROFESSOR VERDIGRIS!

INDEED IT *IS*...

... MOST *REGRETTABLE* THAT YOU WILL NEVER HAVE A CHANCE TO MEET HIM *PROPERLY*.

DAMN...

PLEASE TO STAY STILL, ALL OF YOU. *MOVE*, I KILL HER *FIRST*. NOW *DROP* GUN!

YOU HAVE DONE *WELL*, MR BOX, BUT NOW IT TIME TO STOP *TOYING* WITH YOU!

YOU *DANGLE* LIKE CHILD'S PUPPET.

NOW PLEASE TO BRING PROFESSOR.

3 TO VC...

"... THE PURPLE POPPY..."

PROF. SASH

PROF. QUIBBLE

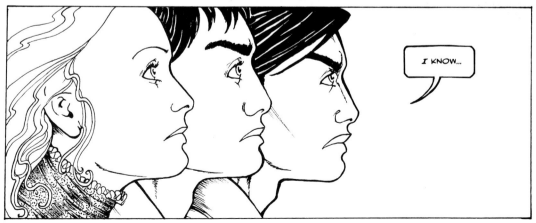

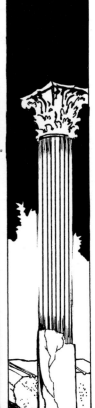

VENUS IS *INSANE!* HE WANTS US ALL HERE FOR HIS ULTIMATE *REVENGE!*

CUT... CABLES...

UHK

GKK –

WHAT *NOW*, MR BOX?

NOW...?

IS... IS THIS TRUE?

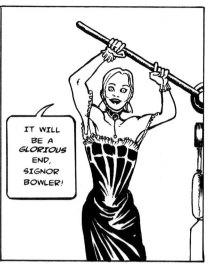

IT WILL BE A *GLORIOUS* END, SIGNOR BOWLER!

WE SHALL TAKE ALL OF ITALY *WITH US!*

KLUNK

CHRIST ALMIGHTY!

HE'S STARTED THE *COUNTDOWN!* THE BOMB'S ALREADY *ROLLING!* THE ONLY WAY TO STOP IT IS TO DETONATE THE BOMB IN THE PIPE *BEFORE* IT REACHES THE *LAVA!*

TIK TIK TIK TIK

"THE CONTROL PANEL..."

CHANG CHANG CHANG CHANG CHANG

KUNG

VERY WELL...

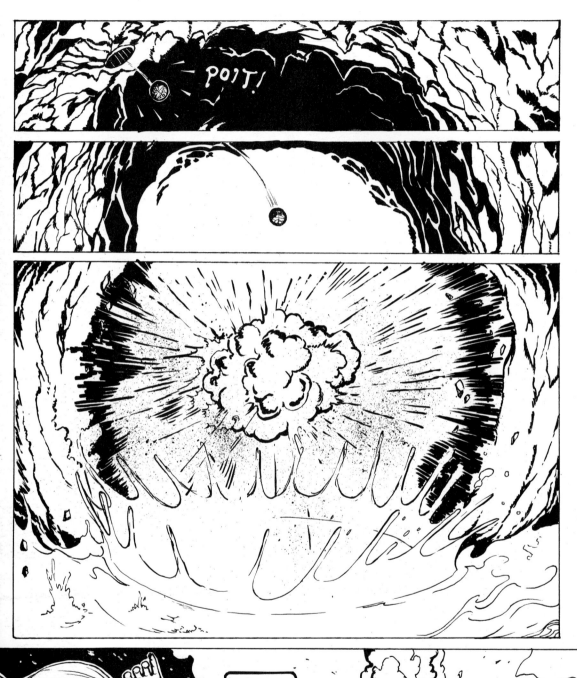

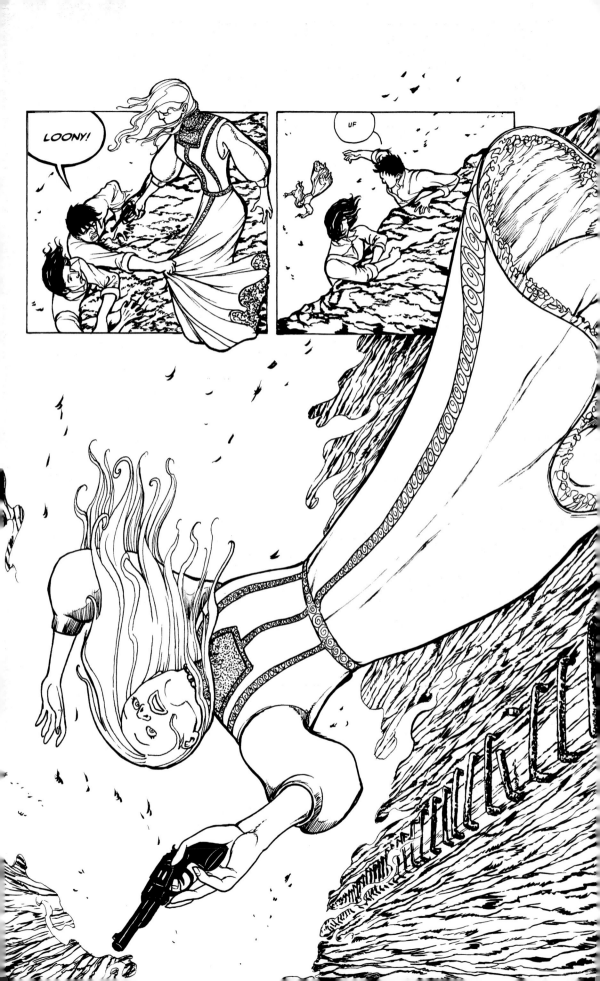

ISSUE No.13

MAY 1939

A THRILLING GIM PUBLICATION

THE WORLD'S MOST EXHILARATING SPY STORIES EVER!

SLEUTH COMICS

10d

FEATURING LUCIFER BOX

SECRET AGENT OF THE EDWARDIAN AGE

MYSTERIOUS SUSPENSE

SPY ADVENTURE

SHOCKING SECRETS

ZOMBIE TERROR!

ACKNOWLEDGEMENTS

HUGE THANKS TO MARK GATISS AND TO GUY BASS. THANKS TO BEN BALL, ROCHELLE VENABLES, JULIA WESTWOOD AND ALL THE TEAM AT SIMON AND SCHUSTER. THANK YOU TO SIMON FURMAN, CLAYTON HICKMAN, ANNECY LAX, ANNA STOKES AND CHRIS AND MORVA BASS.

A SPECIAL THANK YOU TO RUTH GIBSON FOR EXEMPLARY COLOURING IN, TEXTURES, BRICKWORK, AND FOR BEING THE PERFECT BELLA.